D1542437

The Beautifull Cassandra

The Beautifull Cassandra

A Novel in Twelve Chapters

———◆———

Jane Austen

———◆———

Afterword by Claudia L. Johnson
Artwork by Leon Steinmetz

Princeton University Press
Princeton & Oxford

Copyright © 2018 by Princeton University Press
Artwork copyright © 2018 by Leon Steinmetz
Requests for permission to reproduce material from this work
should be sent to permissions@press.princeton.edu
Published by Princeton University Press
41 William Street, Princeton, New Jersey 08540
6 Oxford Street, Woodstock, Oxfordshire OX20 1TR
press.princeton.edu
All Rights Reserved
Library of Congress Control Number: 2018940956
ISBN (pbk.) 978-0-691-18153-0
British Library Cataloging-in-Publication Data is available
Editorial: Anne Savarese and Thalia Leaf
Production Editorial: Terri O'Prey
Text Design: Maria Lindenfeldar
Jacket/Cover Design: Maria Lindenfeldar
Jacket/Cover Credit: Leon Steinmetz
Production: Erin Suydam
Publicity: Julia Haav
This book has been composed in Adobe Caslon Pro
Printed on acid-free paper. ∞
Printed in the Canada
1 3 5 7 9 10 8 6 4 2

Dedicated by permission
to Miss Austen

———◆———

Madam

You are a Phoenix. Your taste is refined, your Sentiments are noble,
& your Virtues innumerable. Your Person is lovely, your Figure, elegant, & your
Form, magestic. Your manners are polished, your Conversation is rational &
your appearance singular. If therefore the following Tale will afford one moment's
amusement to you, every wish will be gratified of

———◆———

your most obedient
humble Servant
The Author

Chapter the First

Cassandra was the Daughter and the only Daughter of a celebrated Millener in Bond Street. Her father was of noble Birth, being the near relation of the Dutchess of —'s Butler.

Chapter the 2ᵈ

When Cassandra had attained her 16th year, she was lovely & amiable & chancing to fall in love with an elegant Bonnet, her Mother had just compleated bespoke by the Countess of —, she placed it on her gentle Head & walked from her Mother's shop to make her Fortune

Chapter the 3ᵈ

The first person she met, was the Viscount of— a young Man, no less celebrated for his Accomplishments & Virtues, than for his Elegance & Beauty. She curtseyed & walked on.

Chapter the 4th

She then proceeded to a Paſtry-cooks, where she devoured six ices, refused to pay for them, knocked down the Paſtry Cook & walked away.

Chapter the 5ᵗʰ

She next ascended a Hackney Coach & ordered it to Hampstead, where she was no sooner arrived than she ordered the Coachman to turn round & drive her back again.

Chapter the 6th

Being returned to the same spot of the same Street she had sate out from, the Coachman demanded his Pay.

Chapter the 7ᵗʰ

She searched her pockets over again & again; but every search was unsuccessfull. No money could she find. The man grew peremptory. She placed her bonnet on his head & ran away.

Chapter the 8ᵗʰ

Thro' many a Street she then proceeded & met in none the least Adventure till on turning a Corner of Bloomsbury Square, she met Maria.

Chapter the 9th

Cassandra started & Maria seemed surprised; they trembled, blushed, turned pale & passed each other in a mutual silence.

Chapter the 10th

Cassandra was next accosted by her freind the Widow, who squeezing out her little Head thro' her less window, asked her how she did? Cassandra curtseyed & went on.

Chapter the 11th

A quarter of a mile brought her to her paternal roof in Bond Street, from which she had now been absent nearly 7 hours.

Chapter the 12th

She entered it & was pressed to her Mother's bosom by that worthy Woman. Cassandra smiled & whispered to herself "This is a day well spent."

Finis.

Afterword

When the British philosopher Gilbert Ryle was asked whether he read novels, he famously replied, without missing a beat, "Oh, yes—all six, every year." And without missing a beat we get the joke, of course, *not* because we believe that Austen's novels throw all others into the shadows (though we do), and *not* because they bear annual rereading (though they do), but rather because we all know—or think we know—that she wrote six of them.

But Austen wrote more than six novels. Along with *Love and Freindship* and *Lady Susan*, which enjoy modest fame, Austen proudly subtitled several shorter works as "A Novel"—such as *Jack and Alice: a Novel* and *Henry and Eliza: a Novel*. But these, though enjoyed by a handful of avid enthusiasts, are mostly unknown to the general public. Written for the amusement of her family, these works belong to the collection of early writing referred to sometimes as the "juvenilia" or "minor works," both terms being rather disparaging, and most recently as "Teenage Writings." Variously described—by Austen herself—as novels, tales, odes, plays, fragments, memoirs, and scraps, the juvenilia consist of twenty-seven pieces written from 1787 to 1793, when Austen was between the ages of eleven and eighteen. Austen was demonstrably attached to these works, in 1793 transcribing them into three stationer's notebooks and entitling them *Volume the First*, *Volume the Second*, *Volume the Third*, each paginated and each including a table of contents. That Austen esteemed these pieces is proven by the very existence of these volumes, presented as if together they might constitute a magnum opus, a three-volume novel in the manner, say, of *Pride and Prejudice* or *Emma*. That she continued to return to these works once she grew up is proven by her emendations in the first two decades of the nineteenth century, and by her allowing a niece and nephew to try their hands at finishing some as late as 1814–16. That Austen's closest relations continued to treasure them is proven by the fact that Austen's sister, Cassandra, the keeper of Austen's literary effects, carefully preserved these volumes after Austen's death, and upon her own willed them to her brothers and her nephew.[1]

Included in *Volume the First*, *The Beautifull Cassandra: A Novel in Twelve Chapters*, written when Austen was twelve, is among the most brilliant and polished of these youthful "novels." Dedicated to

Austen's sister Cassandra, *The Beautifull Cassandra* is the only one of Austen's works with a heroine of this name. We have no direct knowledge of any inside jokes connecting Cassandra Austen to her fictional namesake, but the shared name alone might account for the affection and indulgence with which Austen treats this exceptional heroine, who walks through London much as the two sisters may have during their 1788 visit to that city. Nowadays, we would probably classify *The Beautifull Cassandra* as a tale, sketch, or novella, but Austen's own choice of "novel" says a lot about her sense of humor, to be sure, and also about her ambition. Weighing in at only 465 occasionally misspelled words, each chapter consisting of only one or two sentences, *The Beautifull Cassandra* narrates the wild and slightly criminal adventures of the titular character, as she leaves her maternal roof to flounce around London, eating ice cream (without paying), taking cab rides (without paying), and encountering a handsome young gentleman and lady (without speaking), and all to return home hours later with whispered joy: "This is a day well spent!" A masterpiece of novelistic minimalism, it deserves to be read by everyone who loves Jane Austen, by everyone who loves novels, by everyone who possesses a keen sense of the absurd, by every parent to every child in the interests of cultivating an ear for the cadences of English prose, by everyone who loves a laugh.

Like many of Austen's youthful writings, *The Beautifull Cassandra* experiments vigorously with literary conventions—with dedication, with stock diction, characters, and incidents, with sentence structure, and, of course most strikingly, with chapter length. Indeed virtually every sentence plays parodically upon our expectations concerning what we're reading. Consider Austen's opening gambit, which takes aim at the conventions of literary dedication, notoriously fulsome during the seventeenth and eighteenth centuries. John Dryden, for example, dedicates his *State of Innocence* to the Duchess of York with characteristically labored flattery: "[W]hile You are in sight, we can neither look nor think on any else. There are no Eyes for other Beauties: You only are present . . . Our sight is so intent on the Object of its Admiration, that our Tongues have not leisure even to praise you: for Language seems too low a thing to express your Excellence." Austen follows suit with the ludicrously hyperbolic, if more concise, compliment that opens her dedication to Cassandra. "You are a Phoenix" both explores and explodes the absurd adulation of dedicatory discourse.

Next, the young Austen turns her parodic attention to the formal, tripartite sentence structure so common in eighteenth-century prose:

> Your taste is refined, your Sentiments are noble, & your Virtues innumerable. Your Person is lovely, your Figure, elegant, & your Form, magestic. Your manners are polished, your Conversation is rational & your appearance singular.

Ideally, three-part parallel construction imparts a sense of the writer's intellectual vigor by demonstrating how she or he can pack disparate material into a coherent and dignified whole. Austen spoils the effect by composing three three-part sentences in a row, each marked with the same rhythms, and each employing terms so formulaic as finally to sound perfectly inane.

Since *The Beautifull Cassandra* shows us how exquisitely tuned Jane Austen's ear was to small units of prose at so early an age, it's worth looking even more closely at this style of sentence, which she probes a good deal in her early works. In *Jack and Alice*, for example, she shows how deeply she understands parallel constructions in this description of a character named Lady Williams: "Tho' Benevolent & Candid, she was Generous & sincere; Tho' Pious & Good, she was Religious & amiable, & Tho Elegant & Agreable, she was Polished & Entertaining" (Sabor, 14). Making our way through this complex sentence, we expect to proceed through a series of three finely balanced pairs of antitheses, only to find that Austen has fooled us by presenting us instead with a pair of equivalences, thus obliging us to reread her sentences in order to account for our perplexity. In *The Beautifull Cassandra* Austen is less extravagantly absurd, but she still delights in playing with sentence structure and producing eloquent nonsense: "Your Person is lovely, your Figure, elegant, & your Form, magestic." When we encounter a sentence such as this, we are lulled into supposing that each element in the unfolding series of three will be distinct, yet held together and mastered through the power of parallel structure. But no! Here Austen once again amuses herself by making those three elements—person, figure, and form—virtually synonyms, thus confounding the very purpose of tripartite sentence structure to begin with and turning the whole sentence once again into a joke.

In all these cases, we might say that the very young Jane Austen is having simple fun with the grandiosity of specific words and structures and just leave it at that. But then we have to ask ourselves, what sort of twelve-year-old has already become so well read as to have mastered the weights, rhythms, and registers of the English language? What sort of twelve-year-old already possesses, first, the curiosity to understand how words or sentences or any literary conventions work, and, second, the brilliance and confidence to parody them? For this particular twelve-year-old, parodic imitation is not a means of mockery and dismissal, but rather a means of exploring the properties of any given form, much as, in *Northanger Abbey*, she would both spoof and pay homage to gothic fiction. So, yes, Austen is having fun, but it is not simple fun. It is deep and very smart fun, the kind of fun that emerges from wide and engaged reading, the kind of fun that makes us smart enough to read her properly.

And that is only the beginning. As the novel proceeds, Austen continues to set us up for laughs, making us aware of our assumptions about what happens, and to whom, in novels by thwarting those assumptions. Cassandra is just sixteen when the novel starts, a promising age for Austenian heroines to begin their careers: Catherine Morland is seventeen, Marianne Dashwood sixteen, and Fanny Price is ten when we first meet her and eighteen by novel's end. So Cassandra is the right age for a heroine, though the description of her as "lovely & amiable" might arouse our suspicion by being a bit too pat, too clichéd to be credible, conveying nothing in particular, and less than nothing the more we learn about her. Cassandra has just chanced to "fall in love." This seems to comply with novelistic codes, for aren't all heroines supposed to pine for their heroes? Evidently not, for the object of Cassandra's affection turns out to be a bonnet. That love certainly has a touch of the transgressive about it, for Cassandra no sooner sees the bonnet than she steals it—an act described with playfully highfalutin euphemism as placing it "on her gentle Head" and walking out the door. Unlike most heroines—take Lydia Bennet, for example—Cassandra is indifferent to men. Clad in her beloved bonnet, she takes no interest in the dashing Viscount of —, whom we might have assumed to be the mandatory love interest. But Cassandra has no wish to linger. Instead, she makes a beeline for the pastry shop in order to indulge another passion: ice cream. This she does not, like a true heroine, daintily taste, but downright "devours," and in not one, nor two, nor even three servings, but six. Having sated her appetite, she then "knocks" down the shopkeeper, who demanded his pay, and walks away.

Clearly, Cassandra is no ordinary heroine. A paragon of cheerful irresponsibility, Cassandra regards the world as her oyster. She seizes and enjoys what she wants, and what she wants is not cheap: a bonnet made to order for a countess, according to the latest fashion, would be expensive, and ice cream was a luxury item. She proceeds on her adventures without any care for the scruples of economy that worried eighteenth-century heroines. Indeed, Cassandra has no apparent regard even for the basic rules of law—such as not assaulting or stealing from people—so it should not surprise us that she also flouts the rules of propriety: young ladies should not travel alone, and they definitely should not appear in public without a head covering, as Cassandra does from chapter 7 on. Like Lydia Bennet, whose crime is of a decidedly different nature, Cassandra's unruliness goes entirely

unpunished; but unlike Lydia, Cassandra is permitted to charm us by her unflappable liveliness. *The Beautifull Cassandra* is propelled by its heroine's serial wishes. Each of Cassandra's mini- or nonadventures concludes merely with a determination to have more, much as she wanted one serving of ice cream after another. A kinetic heroine, Cassandra is always on her way somewhere—she "walked away," she "walked on," she "went on, " she "ran away"—always exiting the frame and commencing another chapter.

By Austen's time, the formal unit of the chapter had become so basic to novels that it had ceased to be noticed as the convention it was. This had not been so in Daniel Defoe's novels or in epistolary novels by Samuel Richardson or Eliza Haywood, but virtually all of the later novels that Austen read and enjoyed were structured by chapters. What, then, could Austen have meant by making such a point of drastically reducing the length of her chapters to barely a sentence or two? Given that most of Austen's early writing proceeds from and in turn creates a dazzling formal self-consciousness, exploring the function of conventions, stock characters, and diction by parodying them, it is possible that one of Austen's targets here is the prolixity of popular fiction during her time, which stretched out little matter into long chapters and then into three or five volumes. By conspicuously reversing such practice here, foreshortening her chapters almost to the breaking point, Austen may be asking how many novels could or should be reduced to a sentence or two.

But there is another possible way to account for the spareness of chapters in *The Beautifull Cassandra*. For generations, readers have been divided into two major camps: those who "get" Jane Austen and those who emphatically do not, those who see her richness and complexity and those who see nothing and who accordingly look with a mixture of incredulity and contempt upon those who disagree. "Why do you like Miss Austen so very much? I am puzzled on that point," Charlotte Brontë peevishly asked George Henry Lewes, who admired Austen. More scornfully still, Ralph Waldo Emerson complained, "I am at a loss to understand why people hold Miss Austen's novels at so high a rate . . . Never was life so pinched and so narrow . . . Suicide is more respect-able." And in his infamous "Jane Austen: A Depreci-ation," an address delivered to the Royal Society for Literature in 1928, H. W. Garrod damns Austen as an "irredeemably humdrum" writer, "as incapable of having a story as of writing one—by a story I mean a sequence of happenings, either romantic or uncommon." What bewilders and annoys these readers is the absence of event, or more precisely of what they consider to be interesting, grand, or significant event. For them, nothing happens in Austen's novels: characters and actions alike are ordinary and undramatic.[2]

Unlike *The Beautifull Cassandra*, many of Austen's early works are teeming with remarkable incidents. In the hilarious "Scrap" entitled "A Letter from Young Lady, whose feeling being too Strong for her Judgement led her into the Commission of Errors which her Heart disapprove" from *Volume the Second*, for example, patricide is only the first among the "Errors" committed by the heroine:

I murdered my father at a very early period of my Life, I have since murdered my Mother, and I am now going to murder my Sister. I have changed my religion so often that at present I have not an idea of any left. I have been a perjured witness in every public tryal for these past twelve Years; and I have forged my own will. In short, there is scarcely a crime that I have not committed. (Sabor, 222)

But the best part of this inventory is the sublimely fatuous deadpan with which it concludes: "But I am now going to reform." From homicide we turn to suicide in *Frederic & Elfrida*, where the sweet-tempered Charlotte, "whose nature . . . was an earnest desire to oblige every one," amiably accepts two successive proposals of marriage and is so shocked to recollect her "double engagement" the next morning that she throws herself into a stream and floats, Ophelia-like, back to her village, "where she was picked up and buried" by her friends (Sabor, 9). Alcoholism reigns supreme in *Jack and Alice*, where the principals are often passing the bottle, arguing noisily, and carried home "Dead Drunk" (Sabor, 16). In *Henry and Eliza*, cannibalism makes a cameo appearance, when the heroine, having escaped a dungeon with her two children, "began to find herself rather hungry, and had reason to think, by their biting off two of her fingers, that her Children were in much the same situation" (Sabor, 43). Manifestly Austen could make a lot happen when she wanted to, though of course these overblown events are so ridiculous as to be more likely to irk rather than please any reader in search of "romantic or uncommon" adventures.

The Beautifull Cassandra is markedly different. It is the first novel by Jane Austen fully to embrace the uneventful. True, Cassandra is a tad felonious, but stiffing a pastry chef and a coachman, knocking down the former and plonking her bonnet upon the head of the latter, surely fall short of the passionate adventures that Brontë or Garrod wanted from interesting narrative. Cassandra's ride to Hampstead, for example, is pointedly unremarkable. Her journey there and back takes up no more than a single sentence. No action or encounter or observation emerges from this outing, and she returns immediately to "the same spot of the same Street she had sate out from" for no apparent purpose and to no apparent effect, except for running up her coach fare and obliging her to make a quick escape. When she comes upon the mysterious Maria and they "trembled, blushed, turned pale"—clues that in any other novel of the time would suggest that some conflict has taken place in the past and that some dramatic event is about to transpire—Austen thwarts our desire for an upshot. Nothing happens except more forward movement out of the frame. *The Beautifull Cassandra* thus anticipates Austen's mature novelistic practice by eschewing grandiose adventure. It experiments—in a rather extreme way—with writing on what Austen would later call a "little bit (two inches wide) of ivory," taking that narrowness about which Emerson and others complained and turning it into a rich field for her artistic originality.

What makes *The Beautifull Cassandra* so fabulous and so enduring is its stylistic mastery. Reading Austen's youthful works, only parts of which had just been published, for the first time, Virginia Woolf spotted exactly this quality, remarking that even though Austen's youthful writings surely entertained Austen's family circle, they were meant "to outlast the Christmas holidays." Austen was writing for posterity, even at age eleven: "She was writing for everybody, for nobody, for our age, for her own; in other words, even at that early age Jane Austen was writing."[3] In its wisecracking, experimentation, and parody, the youthful writing shows a stunning audacity, virtuosity, and, most of all, authority. The juvenilia are important, then, not only because they lead to Austen's mature work, but because so many of them are perfect works in their own right, in which Jane Austen first realizes and relishes her status, as she proudly signs herself here, "THE AUTHOR."

———

Austen's novels are sparse in visual details. G. H. Lewes wondered whether Austen was nearsighted, for he found that "the absence of all sense of the outward world—either scenery or personal appearance—is more remarkable in her than in any writer we remember."[4] In this respect *The Beautifull Cassandra* is exceptional, for in addition to being a novel in twelve chapters, *The Beautifull Cassandra* is a series of twelve vignettes, something akin to a graphic novel *avant la lettre*. More than most works by Jane Austen, it seems to call out for some sort of visual counterpart—drawings or *tableaux vivants*.

Leon Steinmetz's series of drawings here answer that call. They are not illustrations of *The Beautifull Cassandra* in any ordinary sense. They make no attempt at historic exactitude regarding Regency period fashion, for example. Maintaining their own contemporary character, they are instead a series of conversations with the text. As conversationalists, Steinmetz's drawings and Austen's novel are splendidly well suited to each other. They are each masterpieces of economy, with only a few sentences on one side, and a few brushstrokes on the other. They are simple-*seeming*, but actually the result of immense virtuosity. They give the effect of breezy, effortless freedom, of being dashed off, but are produced by consummate control. They are intensely stylized, at times almost theatrically so, and of course they are richly comical. And the conversation goes in both directions. Steinmetz's drawings bring out the boldness and the sometimes absurdist modernity of *The Beautifull Cassandra*—as when the pastry chef takes a tumble—while Austen's novel enhances the illustrative qualities in his drawing: note, for example, the six serving dishes of ice cream. At the same time, some of Steinmetz's art brings out a touching quality in the comely Cassandra that is not so apparent in Austen's prose, as in his final drawing, where Cassandra seems to be a less imposing figure at last, and where the maternal embrace seems to be the sweetest of her day's adventures.

Steinmetz's drawings here are similar in style to his commedia dell'arte series, some of which are in the permanent collection at the renowned Pushkin Museum in Moscow and in private collections all over the world. Printed here at their actual size, they are executed with a large Chinese calligraphy brush, using Holbein Ivory Black and Indian Red watercolor paints, on Fabriano, Arches, Winsor & Newton, and Somerset papers. The weight and tooth of the paper are essential for the effect Steinmetz achieves here, where his rapid brushstrokes, imbued with just the right amount of paint, begin wet and fully visible and end dry and faint. This challenging technique gives his images a lively sense of the gestural, of movement through space, and of whimsical freedom, appearing deceptively simple. While the drawings are figural, the use of a calligraphy brush also heightens the abstractness of the images, as in the drawings that accompany chapters 1 and 2, which might momentarily come across as Chinese characters.

In defamiliarizing the adventures of Austen's roguish heroine, Steinmetz's cross-century conversations give Jane Austen back to us. Her work is so familiar to so wide an audience that we have ceased to be amazed by it, to recognize its cheekiness and daring. Sometimes, in fact, Austen's novels almost seem more like museum pieces, meant to inspire hushed tones of admiration, rather than the daring, experimental, and unconventional works they are. After reading *The Beautifull Cassandra* we will no longer be inclined to regard Austen's mature novels as serene or decorous. In the antiheroism of *Northanger Abbey*'s Catherine Morland—who, disappointed, returns home to appease her "extraordinary hunger" and sleep soundly for nine hours, instead of starving herself sleeplessly—we will recognize Cassandra's hearty appetite. In Elizabeth Bennet's dirty petticoats, soiled by her vigorous journey on foot and *alone* through muddy lanes in *Pride and Prejudice* to see her ailing sister, we see Cassandra's readiness to dispense with the rules of propriety. In the comic abruptness with which Austen follows Marianne's enthusiasm for walking in nature—"Is there a felicity in the world . . . superior to this?"—with a very unsentimental rainstorm that cuts short her raptures in *Sense and Sensibility*, we see the same tendency to foil sentimental formulas as in *The Beautifull Cassandra*. And even in Mary Crawford's quip "Nothing ever fatigues me, but doing what I do not like," in *Mansfield Park*, we can see the descendant of Cassandra's animated determination to do whatever she likes, and with similar dodginess.

This edition of *The Beautifull Cassandra* invites readers to see Austen with new eyes, all the better to enjoy the edginess and originality she displays with such exuberance and delight.

A Note on the Text

This edition of *The Beautifull Cassandra* follows Austen's manuscript in *Volume the First* at the Bodleian Library, Oxford, scrupulously edited and digitized by Kathryn Sutherland for *Jane Austen's Fiction Manuscripts Digital Edition* online. I have modernized Austen's long "s" for the ease of the modern reader, but have retained her spelling and punctuation throughout.

Notes

1. For a splendid account of Austen's youthful manuscripts and their uneven journeys from private ownership to publication, see Peter Sabor's authoritative edition, *Juvenilia* (Cambridge: Cambridge University Press, 2006), xxiii–lxvii, a volume in *The Cambridge Edition of the Works of Jane Austen*. Subsequent citations from other works in this volume will be noted parenthetically. I am also indebted to Margaret A. Doody's superlative introduction to *Catharine and Other Writings*, Oxford World's Classics (Oxford: Oxford University Press, 1993). Also see *Jane Austen: Teenage Writings*, ed. Kathryn Sutherland and Freya Johnston, Oxford World's Classics (Oxford: Oxford University Press, 2017).

2. Charlotte Brontë, from a letter to G. H. Lewes, January 12, 1848; Emerson from a journal entry for 1861. Both are cited in B. C. Southam's indispensable *Jane Austen: The Critical Heritage* (London: Routledge & Kegan Paul, 1968), 126, 88. H. W. Garrod's "Jane Austen: A Depreciation" was originally delivered at the Royal Society for Literature in May 1928, and was published in *Essays by Divers Hands: Transactions of the Royal Society of Literature* 8 (1928): 21–40; it has been reprinted in numerous other places. The version quoted here is from William W. Heath, ed., *Discussions of Jane Austen* (Boston: Heath and Company, 1961), 32–40.

3. Virginia Woolf, *The Common Reader. First Series* (New York: Harcourt, 1925), 139. From her review of *Volume the Second*, which was published for the first time under the title of *Love and Friendship and Other Early Works*, ed. G. K. Chesterton (New York: Frederick Stokes Co., 1922). *The Beautifull Cassandra* did not appear until 1933, when *Volume the First* was published.

4. Southam, 159; from G. H. Lewes's unsigned "The Novels of Jane Austen" in *Blackwood's Edinburgh Magazine* 86 (July 1859): 99–113.

Jane Austen (1775–1817) is best known as the author of six novels: *Sense and Sensibility* (1811), *Pride and Prejudice* (1813), *Mansfield Park* (1814), *Emma* (1815), and *Northanger Abbey* and *Persuasion* (both 1818).

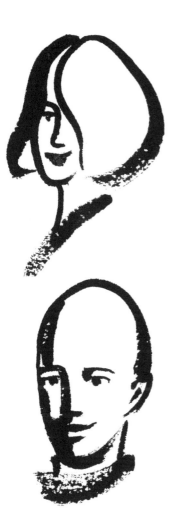

Claudia L. Johnson, Murray Professor of English at Princeton University, is a leading expert on Jane Austen. Her 1988 book, *Jane Austen: Women, Politics, and the Novel*, was hailed as one of the best books ever written on Jane Austen, and her recent book on Austen-love, *Jane Austen's Cults and Cultures* (2012), won the coveted Christian Gauss Prize.

Leon Steinmetz is a contemporary American artist. His art is represented in the permanent collections of the world's major art museums: the Metropolitan Museum of Art, New York; the British Museum, London; the Museum of Fine Arts, Boston; the Philadelphia Museum of Art; the Dresden State Art Gallery; the Yale University Art Gallery, New Haven; the Albertina, Vienna; and the Pushkin State Museum of Fine Arts in Moscow among them, and also in private collections in the United States and Europe. His two latest solo museum exhibits were at the Pushkin State MFA in Moscow: *Steinmetz—Contemplating Gogol* (December 2009–January 2010) and *Leon Steinmetz: The Spell of Antiquity* (July–September 2016).

This deluxe edition of *The Beautifull Cassandra* was composed with
Adobe Caslon Pro and Hoefler Text Ornaments, and it was printed on
Rolland Endleaf 80# paper and Mohawk Via Felt cover stock.

———◆———

We would like to thank the many people at Princeton University Press
who made this book possible. We are particularly grateful to Anne Savarese
and Maria Lindenfeldar, who welcomed our project from the start, who
helped through every stage of its production, and who brought our
design ideas to the printed page.

Special thanks are also due to John Horner, for his brilliant photographs
and for his contributions to our initial design.

———◆———

We dedicate this book to the memory of Inga Karetnikova.